Christmas Tapestry

PATRICIA POLACCO

PHILOMEL BOOKS

There are those who say there is no balance in the universe and that all things happen randomly . . . without purpose. Take, for instance, one Jonathan Jefferson Weeks. He was most upset that his family came all the way from Memphis, Tennessee, when his father accepted the position of pastor at the New Baptist in Detroit. Even though their new home was on the outskirts . . . it was still Detroit! Nothing like Tennessee!

What possible good reason could there be for leaving home and coming here?

Jonathan Jefferson Weeks' father's church in Memphis had been so beautiful—new and gleaming. Everyone had loved to come to his father's services and Jonathan loved his school. He had just made it on the soccer team! And even though he was a "PK," a preacher's kid, his friends there didn't treat him any differently than anyone else.

Here in Detroit, Michigan, his father's new church was practically falling down. It was rickety and old. And the parsonage was right next door.

Here everything about their life screamed . . . PK!

"Why did we come here, Daddy?" Beth asked her father at dinner one night. "The church looks awful. Nobody comes to services."

"The deacons sent your father here because this little church is in such need of new life!" Jonathan's mother said. "Your father made our church in Memphis into something beautiful, didn't he? You should have seen it when we first arrived there!"

"It couldn't have been as bad as this place," Jonathan said.

"Oh, but it was, Jonathan . . . worse!" His father smiled.

Their parents took them into the living room and pulled out a photo album from one of the packing boxes. Jonathan and Beth couldn't believe their eyes. Their father was right. The Tennessee church had been worse . . . far worse!

"How did you do it, Dad?" Jonathan asked.

"Just the way I'm going to do it here. But I need both of you to help me! There's the hard work that it is going to take to repair and rebuild this church. But I'll also need you to be cheerful and brave. When you see what we're going to do to this church, your spirits will be lifted."

Beth and Jonathan tried to smile.

"I predict that by, let's see . . . this very Christmas, the church will be something that we will all be proud of!" their father said. "When it is finished, people will come. You'll see!"

Even though Beth and Jonathan missed Memphis, they threw themselves into the tasks that were assigned to them.

For that whole summer they both helped clear out trash, cut back bushes, mow the lawns and plant bulbs for the next spring. They scrubbed floors, washed walls and even helped with the painting. When school started, they were so involved with the rebuilding of the church, they didn't even miss their old friends. They were making new ones.

By fall, not only was the church looking better, but Sunday services were getting more and more crowded. Jonathan's father was just what this neighborhood needed. Folks were very friendly now, and everyone was anxious to help.

Even Jonathan's new classmates came to help paint.

It seemed that everything that the neighbors and friends and family did was turning the church into a beautiful place!

As fall stretched into winter, the church was almost finished. Jonathan's father was right . . . it would be perfect for Christmas.

"Here, Dad," Jonathan said as he handed up a loaded paintbrush to his father on the stepladder one December day.

Reverend Weeks dabbed the last spot of paint on the sacristy wall. "There! Now the artist can paint the wonderful scene we've planned," he said. "It's going to be a glorious painting of our Lord."

Jonathan could hardly wait to see the painting. And it would be done in time for Christmas Eve.

Jonathan walked over to the window and watched the snow steadily falling outside. "I've heard that a blizzard may be coming, Dad . . . and here in Michigan, a blizzard can be real bad!"

"I've heard that, too, but the parsonage is warm and cozy and so is our new church," Reverend Weeks said as he hugged Jonathan. "It won't bother us, will it!"

That next week brought the worst snow that had been seen in Detroit in twenty-five years!

One morning, Mr. Brown, the caretaker, knocked at the parsonage door. He looked full of dread. "Reverend Weeks, come quickly!"

Jonathan, Beth and their parents rushed next door. As they entered the church, they all gasped. A dark water stain covered the sacristy wall . . . right where the painting of our Lord was to be.

"Ice built up on the edge of the roof and held back water," Mr. Brown said sadly. "Standing water, that ran into the building and down the sacristy wall."

"How can this be happening?" Mrs. Weeks cried. "The artist we commissioned to do the painting was going to start tomorrow!"

"Isn't there anything we can do?" the reverend asked Mr. Brown.

"We can chip the ice to let out the standing water on the roof." He lightly pushed at the watery wall. There was a huge crack, a rush of water, and a piece of plaster fell with a thud.

"Dad!" Jonathan cried out. "Now there's a big ugly hole in the wall . . . right where everybody will see it. I even see wooden slats."

"I know a plasterer, Mr. Zukor. He'll be able to fix it for us," Mr. Brown said.

"Before Christmas Eve?" Jonathan asked, full of hope.

"No, sir!" Mr. Brown said. "This here wall needs to dry out first. The plastering may not be until spring."

"I knew something would spoil our Christmas!" Jonathan cried.

"Now, now. I'll call Mr. Zukor anyway. He may have a different solution," Mr. Brown added softly.

Later that night, Reverend Weeks sat on the edge of Jonathan's bed.

"I miss home!" Jonathan cried. "I know you believe God always has a plan, but what plan could have brought us here?" Jonathan sobbed. "We worked so hard, then God sent a blizzard. I don't understand."

"Well, son, although we don't always understand, the universe unfolds as it should," his father said as he rocked the boy in his arms. "Tomorrow will be another day, and perhaps things won't seem so bleak when you wake up to a new morning." Then he kissed the boy good night and closed the door.

T he next morning, Jonathan awoke to a cold snap and freezing snow. His mother asked his father and him to drive to Detroit to pick up Christmas decorations that she had ordered from Horrocks. Jonathan didn't want to go. He felt so bad about the church wall. What good would decorations do?

Then, as if the damage to the church wasn't bad enough, the battery was dead in the family car. "It's all right, Jonathan. We can take the bus."

Jonathan's face fell. The slow old bus all the way downtown and back?

"Why do we need decorations—the church is ruined. Everybody will just sit and look at a hole in the wall," Jonathan said as they boarded the bus.

Downtown, Jonathan and his father slogged through freezing snow. The wind stung their faces.

After they had picked up the decorations, they stepped into an alley to get out of the bitter wind. It wasn't an alley, really, because it was lined by odd little shops. Antiques mostly. Jonathan and his father leaned against one of the windows and caught their breath for a moment.

Jonathan turned toward the window, and that's when he saw it! There was the most beautiful-looking piece of cloth that Jonathan had ever seen! "Dad, look!" Jonathan pulled his father to see.

"Isn't it magnificent!" his father said.

"Wait. If that cloth is big enough, couldn't we buy it and hang it over the hole in the wall?" Jonathan pleaded. "The colors even look like Christmas!"

"Sorry, son, I have fifteen dollars and some change for the bus. That cloth looks like it would cost more than I can afford." He looked in the boy's eyes, so disappointed now. "Well, we can at least go in and look."

The shopkeeper spread the beautiful cloth out on a table.

"Look, Jonathan, hand-stitched embroidery!" Reverend Weeks said as he gazed at the cloth.

"And the perfect size, Dad—see!" Jonathan said as he touched it.

Reverend Weeks looked up. "How much is this?" he asked timidly.

"I've had that old piece here for over a year. For you, Pastor, I'll make a deal. How's fifteen bucks sound?"

"That would be fine, perfectly fine!" Reverend Weeks beamed as the storekeeper wrapped the beautiful tapestry in brown paper.

"Jonathan, you had an inspired idea!" his father said to him as they made their way to the bus stop.

Jonathan and his father waited and waited at the bus stop. The wind burned as it stirred up waves of crystal snow.

Reverend Weeks stepped into the street and leaned out to see if the bus was coming. But there was no sign of it.

"Do you think that the weather is so bad, they've stopped the bus service?" Jonathan asked his father.

"No, it's just late. I'm sure it's just late!" his father reassured.

Jonathan shivered with the bitter cold.

"It's always late!" A voice came out of the white misty snow.

There on the bench was an old lady. "The bus, it's always late!" she said again as she motioned toward town.

Reverend Weeks smiled at her.

Jonathan tried to stand behind his father, out of the bitter wind.

"In my country, winters are worse than this—like a razor the wind cuts. I have hot tea in my thermos and some raisin cookies, too!" she said as she motioned them to sit with her. "Have some with me . . . I would like nothing more this day, than to share a little warm tea with you and your boy!"

Jonathan looked at his father. "Please!" he whispered.

"We're much obliged, ma'am!" Reverend Weeks said as he tipped his hat. The hot tea and the cookies made the wind seem to disappear.

"How far do you have to go today—that is, if the bus ever gets here!" Jonathan asked the lady.

"Well, first the Fifty-two . . . then two transfers before I'll be home," she answered.

"Ma'am, if this bus comes, the way is shorter to my house," Reverend Weeks said. "I have to drop off this package at my church, but I have a car there. By now the battery is charged. I would be pleased, indeed, to take you home in return for your kindness."

"In this cold . . . I will accept. I surely will!" she said with a broad smile.

"If the bus ever comes!" the three of them said in unison, then laughed.

The bus finally did come and the three of them rode through a light snow to Reverend Weeks' church to drop off the package. Mrs. Weeks made more hot tea and shared some special cakes, too.

"Can we put the cloth up, Dad—before we go—just to see what it will look like?" Jonathan pleaded. He could hardly wait.

"I'm in no hurry." The old woman smiled.

Jonathan and his father hung the cloth right over the gaping hole.

"Our Christmas Tapestry," Jonathan announced.

The old lady gasped. "Where did you get this?" she asked breathlessly. She looked pale as snow.

"From an antique store—just before we met you!" Jonathan said to her.

The old lady walked up to the cloth, took out a pair of glasses and looked at it closely.

"I made this!" she said in a whisper. Tears streamed down her face. "In Germany . . . almost sixty years ago. I sewed it with my own hands." She held the cloth with her gnarled fingers. "My applique . . . my family symbols . . . there—do you see, child?"

"Are you sure?" Reverend Weeks asked. This was impossible!

She lifted one of the corners, looked, then sighed. "Those are my initials." Jonathan could see three letters. "I stitched them there myself when I was about to become a bride."

Reverend Weeks started to take the tapestry down. "Surely, then, you should have this blessed cloth back!"

The woman thought for a moment, then moved away. "No . . . here it belongs. Somehow it has made a journey all the way from Germany. It is meant to be here on your wall . . . in this place . . . in this time. I can feel it." Her voice trailed off.

She took her seat again and sipped her tea.

"Many years ago when I married, this was used as my wedding *Chuppah*—the canopy over me and my beloved. Then it was the coverlet on our marriage bed. If there had been children, they would have all been wrapped in this to be named." Her voice trailed off again, then her jaw tightened.

"But then the Nazis came. My people were rounded up—herded like animals. The SS came first for our neighbors . . . and finally for us."

"What happened?" Jonathan asked as he squeezed his father's hand.

"When they came, my young husband was torn from my arms. We were separated. All the women and children were thrown into one railroad car . . . the men and boys into another.

"I shall never forget his sweet eyes, the way he looked at me. I never saw him again. We were all sent to concentration camps. . . ." She pulled up her sleeve and showed a row of faded blue numbers on the inside of the lower arm.

"I'm speechless. No words can describe!" Reverend Weeks said as the whole family leaned toward the lady.

Jonathan beamed as he looked into his father's face. Then he hugged the old woman.

"Would you stay for prayer services tonight," Reverend Weeks suddenly asked, "and have supper with us, too?"

"I'm honored you ask, but I am not of your faith," the old woman said. "Tonight I will say my own prayers, light the menorah and share some of your lovely tea cakes with my cats! But another time I would love to share a feast with you."

"Do you have family to share your holidays?" Reverend Weeks worried.

"No husband—I never married again, but I do have nieces and nephews here in Detroit."

"We shall cherish this wondrous tapestry . . . and even if our wall is repaired, we shall keep this hanging here to commemorate your memories, dear lady!" Reverend Weeks whispered.

The whole family drove home with her.

It was Christmas Eve. There was to be a pageant. Jonathan was going to be a shepherd in the procession of the Christ Child. Beth and her mother were practicing their hymns for the choir. The service was to commence promptly at six o'clock.

That morning there was a knock at the front door. Mr. Brown had brought the plasterer to inspect the damage.

"We didn't expect you to come on such short notice—and especially on Christmas Eve!" Reverend Weeks said as he shook the man's hand.

"Zukor . . . Joachim Zukor," the old man said. "For me it is the Festival of Lights. . . . I live alone, no one will miss me today," Mr. Zukor said with a warm smile.

"This is where the damage is," Reverend Weeks said as they all entered the church together.

Reverend Weeks pulled the tapestry back so that the old man could see the hole in the wall.

Mr. Zukor put on his glasses and inspected the damage very carefully.

"This won't be difficult—not difficult at all!" he said. "You do need to let the wall dry a bit . . . but I can make it look like new!"

"I'm glad to hear that. We were all so worried that the damage was structural!" Reverend Weeks said. He let the tapestry cascade back in front of the hole.

The old man staggered back. "Where did you get this—where . . ."

"Right here in Detroit—" Jonathan tried to explain.

"It couldn't possibly be," Mr. Zukor interrupted.

"Couldn't be what?" Jonathan asked.

"My bride . . . in the old country," Mr. Zukor said softly. "She made something exactly like this for our wedding. Every stitch and pattern . . . all the same." Mr. Zukor started to cry.

"But she was taken by the Nazis. We all were—" he said breathlessly. "We were herded like sheep into boxcars and taken to camps . . . work camps, they called them, but they were a place of death. I never saw her again. She did not survive that place."

Jonathan looked in astonishment at his father and mother. "Did she embroider her initials in the cloth?" Reverend Weeks asked.

"Why . . . yes, yes she did. How did you know that?" Mr. Zukor asked.

Jonathan pulled up the lower corner. Mr. Zukor started sobbing.

"RHZ. Those are her initials. Rachel Hannah Zukor!" the old man said as he collapsed into the first pew.

"Mr. Zukor . . . she's alive. She was just here three days ago. We know right where she is!" Jonathan said as he hugged Mr. Zukor.

The Weeks family drove like the wind with their precious cargo, Mr. Zukor. When they arrived in front of the redbrick apartment house where the old lady lived, the old man flew to the outside door, then climbed three flights of stairs as if he were floating. Jonathan and Beth were out of breath.

Mr. Zukor stopped in front of number 22. He waited for the longest time. Then he knocked. The door opened.

There the old woman stood, puzzled.

Her eyes widened. Then, her eyes brimming, she took his face in her hands. "Is that you, my beloved?" she whispered. "I have waited a long time."

"My Rachel . . . my Rachel!" was all Mr. Zukor could manage to say.

Then a sound came from both of them that Jonathan knew he would never hear the likes of again. It was the sound of joy!

Then they hugged and cried and kissed each other so tenderly that Jonathan didn't really know why but he felt tears in his own eyes.

Later that night at the Christmas Eve services, the candles were radiant. Their flickering light made the tapestry shimmer as if it were enchanted. Maybe it is, Jonathan thought as he smiled to himself. He couldn't take his eyes off of it.

The pageant was beautiful, the church was full of people singing praises. The lights on the Christmas tree reminded Jonathan of the twinkling stars in the night sky.

Jonathan Jefferson Weeks thought his heart would burst at the pure joy of the season . . . and the wonder of all the events that had taken place.

Now he knew exactly why they moved to Detroit exactly when they did. He knew why the plaster fell, why the car didn't start . . . why it was so bitter and cold that he and his father had shared tea with a lonely old woman.

It was all so seamless, woven so perfectly.

Woven as beautifully and surely as Jonathan's radiant cloth that hung at the front of his church.

It was all, truly, a Christmas Tapestry.

for Steven and Leah

Patricia Polacco adapted this story from a tale she has heard in homilies—once in the 1960s from Dr. Clarence Riedenbach of the Oakland Ecumenical Council, and once in the 1990s on Robert Schuller's *Hour of Power*. Both presentations were told as a true stories involving young ministers, one from Canada, the other New York. Ms. Polacco has adapted the tale for young readers and changed the setting to her home state of Michigan.

PATRICIA LEE GAUCH, EDITOR

PHILOMEL BOOKS,
a division of Penguin Putnam Books for Young Readers, 345 Hudson Street, New York, NY 10014.
Philomel Books, Reg. U.S. Pat. & Tm. Off. Published simultaneously in Canada. Manufactured in China by South China Printing Co. Ltd.

Book design by Semadar Megged. The text is set in Adobe 15-point Jenson Regular. The illustrations are rendered in pencil and watercolor.
Library of Congress Cataloging-in-Publication Data   Polacco, Patricia. Christmas tapestry / Patricia Polacco.— 1st ed.   p. cm.   Summary: A tapestry that is being used to cover a hole in a church wall at Christmas brings together an elderly couple who were separated during World War II.
[1. Christmas—Fiction. 2. Jews—Fiction.] I. Title. PZ7.P75186 Cj 2002 [Fic]—dc21 2001007392 ISBN 0-399-23955-3 5 7 9 10 8 6 4